MY BROTHER, MATTHEW

MARY THOMPSON

WOODBINE HOUSE 1992

Library of Congress Cataloging-in-Publication Data

Thompson, Mary, date.
My brother, Matthew / written and illustrated by Mary Thompson.
p. cm.
Summary: Though David knows frustration and resentment at times, he feels he understands his disabled little brother even better than his parents; and together the two boys experience a great deal of joy.
ISBN 0–933149–47–6 : $14.95
[1. Brothers—Fiction. 2. Handicapped—Fiction.] I. Title.
PZ7.T37168My 1992
[Fic]—dc20 92–9858
CIP
AC

Manufactured in Hong Kong

10 9 8 7 6 5 4

My brother, Matthew, loves cats. Sometimes on Saturdays we tour our neighborhood looking for cats. It's a slow tour because Matthew insists on a long visit with every cat we find. At first I thought he liked them all the same, but now I know that he especially likes the calico cat across the street.

It took people a while to figure out that the calico cat is Matthew's favorite, because my brother can't speak the way most kids can. But I can understand what he says.

"There's my cat," Matthew says whenever he sees the calico cat.

The calico cat isn't really his cat. It belongs to our neighbor. But the first time my brother said that, I knew it was his favorite.

Besides speaking differently, my brother also moves and sometimes behaves differently than most kids do. That's because he was born with disabilities.

I remember when Matthew was born.

Mom and Dad were always at the hospital with him. But I had to stay home and do jigsaw puzzles with Grandma. Nobody would tell me what was going on.

At last I got to look at my brother through a little window in the hospital hallway. Inside I could see my mom, dressed in a green hospital gown. She was bent over something with tubes and wires which connected to machines and tanks and blinking lights.

That something was my brother, hardly looking like a baby under all that equipment. I finally saw that he was wearing a diaper, as every baby should. Then I began to believe that he *could* be my baby brother.

"What are those tubes and things for?" I asked Dad.

"They help your brother breathe and eat and stay warm, David," he said. "He can't do those things for himself the way most babies can."

"Why not?" I asked. "What happened?"

"Nobody knows for sure," Dad said.

My brother was still in the hospital on my birthday. And Grandma was still staying at our house to help out. Things were pretty tense at home.

Grandma said, "Everything that happens has a purpose, and we have been chosen to care for a special child."

"Nonsense," said Dad. "These kinds of things just happen."

All I knew for sure was that no one was talking about my birthday.

Then, just as Grandma was starting to light the birthday candles, the phone rang.

"That was your mother," said Dad. "Your brother has taken a turn for the worse."

Dad rushed off to the hospital.

When he returned, much later, Dad told me the doctors said my brother was out of danger for now.

But it was too late for a birthday party.

One night Dad told us that he and Mom had decided on a name for my brother: Matthew.

"That's a good name," said Grandma. "It means 'a special gift.'"

Dad just sort of sighed. "Special gift or not," he said, "Matthew still needs to stay in the hospital."

"Why?" I asked. "Isn't he getting better?"

"We're hoping so," Dad said.

"Will he come home soon?" I asked.

"We don't know," said Dad.

I was tired of waiting and I was worried. I didn't know what would happen to my brother. It seemed like most of my questions weren't answered. The answers I got didn't make much sense to me. I just wanted Mom and Matthew home.

Finally, Matthew could breathe and eat and keep warm by himself, and Mom and Dad brought him home from the hospital. I got to hold my brother at last.

Mom sat on one side of me and Grandma on the other.

"Be careful," said Mom.

"Don't drop him," said Grandma.

What did they think I was? An idiot?

Even though he looked like he was asleep, I was sure that he knew who was holding him. And *he* wasn't worried.

I was so relieved to have Mom and Matthew home. Now that we were all together our family would be like a normal family. But Mom said my brother would still need lots of extra care.

Mom said that we had to learn even more about how to care for my brother so he would grow and develop as best he could.

A special person, called a therapist, started coming to our house. She talked to my mom about how to take care of Matthew and showed her exercises to do with him. She brought special toys and games and pieces of equipment for him.

I was supposed to play quietly by myself while she and my mom talked and worked with Matthew. I tried to build my space station, but it was pretty hard with those new toys around. I wanted to play with the special toys, but they were just for Matthew.

Every day, all day long it seemed, Mom was busy with my brother. She played the special games with the new toys. She did the special exercises with him. Mom even bought some cassette tapes with music to use along with the exercises. Pretty soon the tapes were going most of the day. I moved my space station into my bedroom and closed the door. It was better to be a little lonely than to have to listen to those tapes one more time.

Whenever Mom wasn't working with my brother, she was reading about new things to try with him. Mom decided that swimming would be good for my brother, so we went to the pool.

"Watch me dive," I yelled.

"Don't splash Matthew!" Mom shouted at me just before I hit the water. But when I came up, Matthew was smiling and splashing in all directions. He liked my dive.

One day I decided to tell my brother about my space station.

"Watch this!" I said. I launched a moon rocket.

From the look in his eyes, I could tell he liked my space station. So I showed him more, about the robot arms and the deep-space telescope, too. Then he laughed a really happy laugh, his first one.

Mom was excited. I was excited too, but not surprised. I knew the first time I held him that he was a lot like me. I knew that he would like space travel as much as I do.

"Since Matthew likes you so much, maybe you could help with his therapy program," Mom said to me. That's what she called his special exercises.

Therapy program! That sounded like about as much fun as cleaning my bedroom. I decided that I would rather just play with him.

When Matthew was small, he would play almost anything with me. He wasn't like my friends, who usually knew exactly what they did and did not want to play.

"Want to play space explorers?" I asked.

Matthew agreed.

So I pushed him through the house in my cardboard-box spacecraft.

"Slow down a little, David! That's too fast for Matthew," Mom said. Matthew just grinned and shouted for me to go faster.

Now that he is older, my brother has some ideas of his own. Instead of space explorers he often wants to play his own games, like cats in outer space.

Sometimes I read to my brother. This was one of Grandma's ideas when she was here for another visit.

"Why don't you read to Matthew, David? That would be nice and quiet," said Grandma.

So I started to read him my book on alien invaders. Whenever I read "Kaboom!" Matthew wiggled and snuggled closer.

"Oh, dear!" said Grandma. "You'll frighten Matthew with stories like that. Then he'll never settle down and go to sleep."

When I finished the book, I asked Matthew, "How did you like the story?" But Matthew had fallen asleep in my lap.

My mom was the first to notice how well I can understand the way my brother talks. When my family has trouble understanding what Matthew is saying, they ask me to help.

"Orange juice," Matthew says, about six times.

"What did he say, David?" asks Dad.

"He said orange juice. Matthew wants some orange juice," I answer.

"Block!" Matthew says.

"What did he say, David?" asks Grandma.

"He wants a block."

I don't know why they can't understand what he says.

Dad said that it is almost like being an interpreter. But I think that I have just had lots of practice listening to my brother talk on our space radio.

Playing with my brother isn't *always* easy. And sometimes living with him doesn't seem fair.

For example, once we were playing with blocks.

"Look at my moon lander," I called to Mom and Dad.

But no one noticed my moon lander. Matthew had just made his first block tower.

Later my brother used his tower to knock down my moon lander and everyone clapped. Did anyone notice my moon lander was destroyed in the process?

My brother copies me all the time. If I read a book, he picks up a book. If I play with blocks, he wants to play with blocks. If I draw a picture, he starts to draw too.

One time I wanted to play by myself with my dinosaurs. "Mom, tell him not to copy me!" I shouted.

"He copies you because he thinks you're the greatest person in the world, David," Mom replied. "You should be flattered." But I still thought it was annoying.

My brother is always tagging along when I want to play with my friends.

"Dad, Matthew is bothering us," I complained once.

"Maybe you can find a place for Matthew in your game, too," my dad said.

"I'm the cat!" shouted Matthew.

"Matthew wants to be the cat," I explained to my friends. Matthew started meowing and purring like mad. Oh great, I thought. But my friends didn't mind.

Sometimes my brother really embarrasses me. When he came to my class play with Mom and Dad, he made a big noise whenever I was on stage. At the library my brother is never quiet about picking out his books. And, when we eat out at a restaurant, he always spills his milk.

My best friend says it's just the same in his family, and his brother doesn't even have disabilities.

Maybe living with my brother is a lot like living with any other brother, but it can be hard.

My brother has to work more than other kids do to learn new things. He needs extra help from Mom and Dad, and other people, too. We all clap and cheer when he learns something new, and my brother is so happy that he claps too.

But sometimes Matthew doesn't understand or can't do something. Then he feels sad. I am sad, too. When I was younger, I used all my birthday wishes and new star wishes just wishing that my brother could be like other kids. Now I know that wishing won't make it so.

But then there are times when we are not sure he'll ever learn how to do something. And then one day he does. Like no one knew if Matthew would *ever* walk. Mom worked and worked on his exercises. Then one day, when everyone had just about given up, he walked.

The other day I asked my mom, "When will Matthew learn to ride a bike? Then we can go twice as fast on our cat walks."

"We're not sure that Matthew will ever be able to ride a bicycle," Mom answered.

"And if he can ride," added Dad, "we don't know if it will be a regular bicycle or a bike built for riders with special needs."

I sort of think Matthew will learn to ride a bike. But if he does, I don't really know how much faster our cat tour will go. You see, the calico cat just had six kittens.